Two Hoots
and the King

by Helen Cresswell

illustrated by Martine Blanc

Crown Publishers, Inc., New York

First published in the United States in 1978
Text copyright ©1977 by Helen Cresswell
Illustrations copyright ©1977 by Martine Blanc-Rérat
ISBN: 0-517-53494-0

Big Hoot and Little Hoot
lived in the woods.
All of the other owls were
wise, but Big Hoot and
Little Hoot were not.
They were silly.

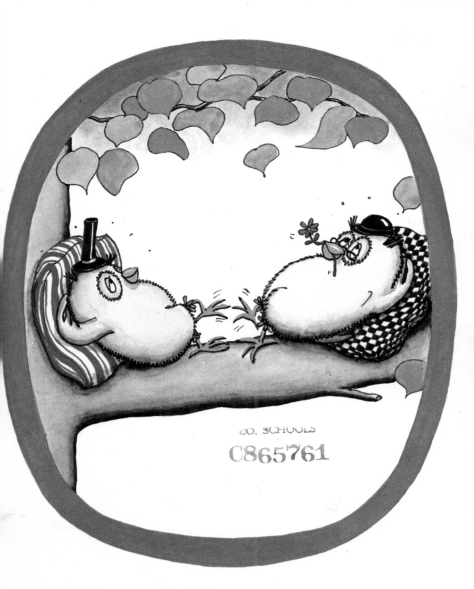

They flew in the
woods during the day.
The wise owls slept
during the day.
The wise owls said,
"Go to sleep,
Big Hoot and Little Hoot.
Be wise, like us!"

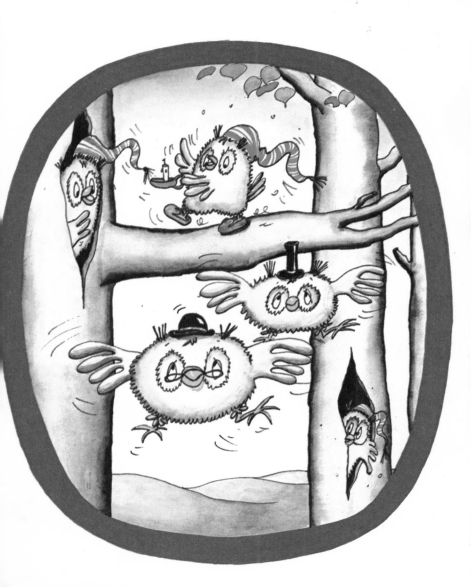

"I would like to be wise,"
   said Big Hoot.
"So would I," said
   Little Hoot.
"I don't like being so silly.
   But I cannot help it."

"Look! Look there!"
said Big Hoot.
They looked. They saw
a little bird.
It was a little
yellow bird.
It was singing.

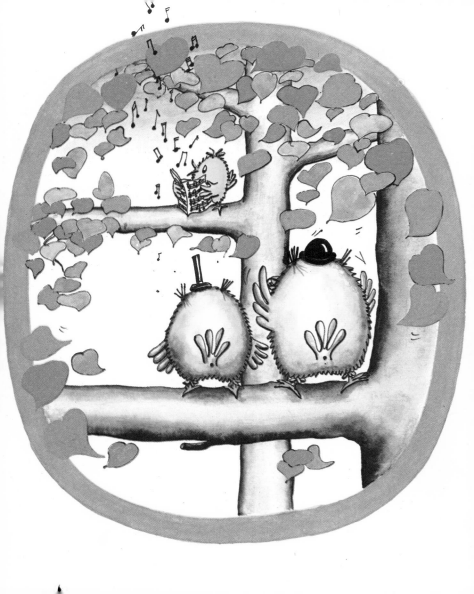

"Do you see what I see?"
said Big Hoot.
"I see a yellow bird,"
said Little Hoot.
"It must be from the sun.
The sun is yellow, and
so is the singing bird."

"And the sun is king of
   the day," said Big Hoot.
"So the yellow bird must
   be king of the sun!"
"Shall we wake all the other
   owls?" asked Little Hoot.
"Then they can see
   the king of the sun."

"No," said Big Hoot.
"Let's ask the sun king
  to give us a wish."
"What wish?" asked Little Hoot.
"Let's ask him to make
  us wise," said Big Hoot.

"What a good idea!"
said Little Hoot.
"How happy I will be
when I am wise.
I shall say wise things
all day and all night!"
"Not all day," said Big Hoot.
"When you are a wise owl,
you will sleep in the day."

Big Hoot and Little Hoot flew
to the little yellow bird.
He was singing.
"Good day, king of the sun,"
said Big Hoot.
"We are happy to know you."
The yellow bird looked
at them.

"We know you are
   king of the sun,"
   said Little Hoot.
"We can see that.
   You are yellow like the sun.
   We would like you to
   give us a wish."
"What wish can I give you?"
   asked the yellow bird.

"Can you make us wise?"
asked Big Hoot.
"Can you help us to be wise,
like the other owls?"
"I can help make you a little
wiser than you are now,"
said the yellow bird.

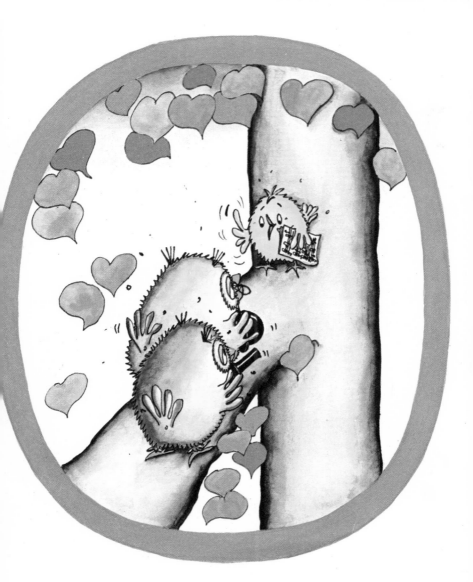

"Good! Good!"
The two Hoots flew to
the other owls.
"Come and see us made
wise!" they said.
The other owls went
to see the singing
yellow bird.

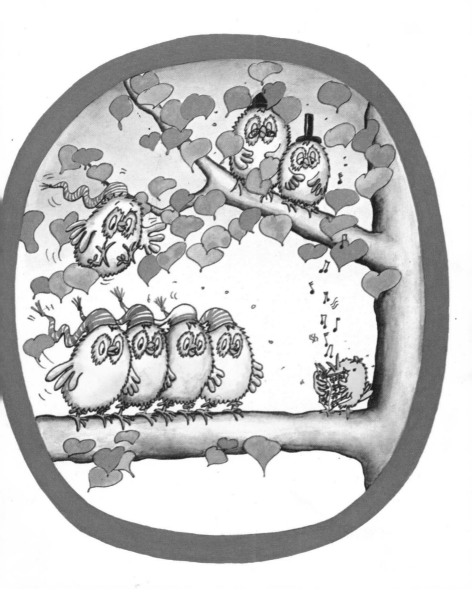

The yellow bird looked at
Big Hoot and Little Hoot.
"I am not king of the sun,"
said the yellow bird.
"I am a canary!
Now you are a little
wiser than you were before!"
He flew away.
"Silly owls!" said
the other owls.
"Go to sleep."
And they did.

OTHER EARLY READERS

Two Hoots

Two Hoots Go to the Sea

Two Hoots and the Big Bad Bird

Two Hoots Play Hide-and-Seek

Two Hoots in the Snow

Two Hoots and the King

10 9 8 7 6 5 4 3 2 1

Library of Congress Cataloging in Publication Data
Cresswell, Helen.   Two hoots and the king.
(An early reader) Summary: The two Hoots request the gift of wisdom from a small yellow bird they are convinced is the king of the sun. [1. Owls—Fiction] I. Blanc, Martine. II. Title. III. Series. PZ7.C8645Tr 1978 [E] 78-55548
ISBN 0-517-53494-0